THE THREE KINGDOMS

LUO GUANZHONG

www.realreads.co.uk

Retold by Christine Sun
Illustrated by Shirley Chiang

Published by Real Reads Ltd
Stroud, Gloucestershire, UK
www.realreads.co.uk

First published in 2011

ISBN 978-1-906230-35-7

Printed in Singapore by Imago Ltd
Designed by Lucy Guenot
Typeset by Bookcraft Ltd, Stroud, Gloucestershire

CONTENTS

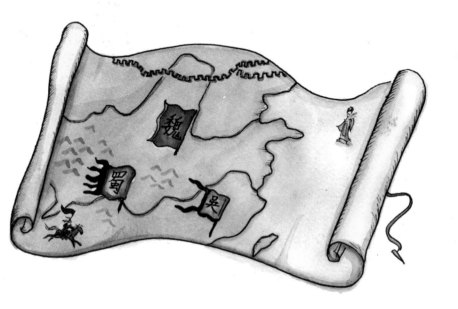

THE CHARACTERS

Liu Bei, Zhang Fei and Guan Yu

These three sworn brothers are committed to serving their country and people, but can they save the Han Empire from destruction?

Zhuge Liang

Zhuge's talents in politics, economics, diplomacy and military manipulation are peerless. Will his schemes to defeat the empire's enemies succeed?

Cao Cao

Military officer Cao is hard to trust and always seems ready to let his friends down. Can he really succeed in becoming the emperor?

Sun Jian, Sun Ce and Sun Quan

Sun Jian and his sons are devoted to establishing their own empire. How are they going to compete against the other warlords?

Zhou Yu

A brilliant scholar, Zhou is gifted in music, literature, politics and military strategies. Can his goals be achieved before he dies?

Sima Yi

Sima is a cunning government official, suspicious of everyone around him. Can he succeed in his quest to gain high office?

Limerick County Library

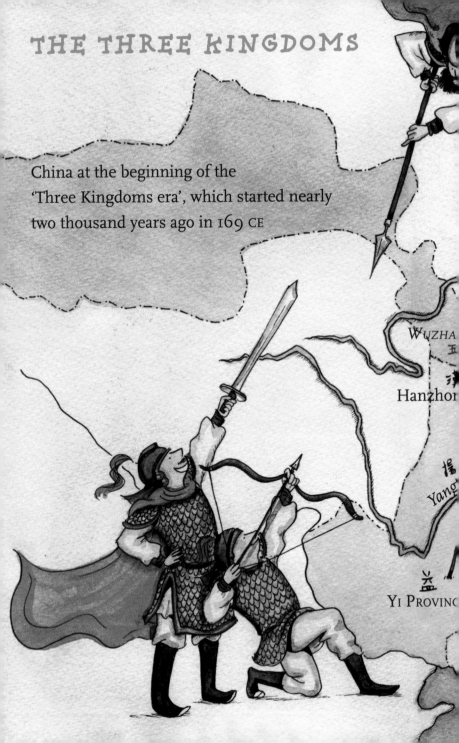

THE THREE KINGDOMS

China at the beginning of the 'Three Kingdoms era', which started nearly two thousand years ago in 169 CE

Wuzha

Hanzhor

Yang

Yi Provinc

THE THREE
KINGDOMS

The great Han Empire was in trouble.

The emperor's servants were regularly deceiving him; any official who was faithful to the emperor was sacked. The government had become corrupt at every level. As a result, the people suffered greatly.

Across the empire riots broke out. Among the most violent protestors were the Yellow Turbans, who claimed to have magical powers. The emperor sent his troops to suppress them, but failed. It was now the responsibility of each province to defend itself.

In Yu Province in the empire's north, the officials decided to put up an announcement to enlist civilian support. Among those who stopped by the public noticeboard was Liu Bei, a handsome young man with unusually long arms and large earlobes. Liu had grown up believing that one should always be loyal to one's country and people. Deeply concerned about the empire's future, he gave a great sigh.

A voice boomed behind him. 'What are you moaning about? Why don't you volunteer to serve your empire!'

Liu turned and saw a large man built like a tower, his face half covered by a dark beard and his eyes blazing with fury.

'I want to fight the Yellow Turbans, but I have neither money nor power,' Liu answered, undaunted by the man's size.

The anger in the man's eyes was replaced with friendly understanding. 'Well, I have money,' he responded, reaching out a hand the size of a dinner plate to shake Liu's. 'My name is Zhang Fei, the town's butcher. I'm not a powerful man, but I can help you.'

Liu and Zhang agreed to have a drink in a nearby tavern. No sooner had they ordered than they heard a fellow drinker yelling at the waiter, 'Give me some wine! Send me off to fight the Yellow Turbans!' This man, whose name turned out to be Guan Yu, was just as imposing as Zhang. His long, lush black beard gave him a dignified look. If Zhang looked like a roaring lion, then Guan resembled a majestic tiger.

Liu and Zhang engaged Guan in conversation, and were delighted to hear that he too wanted to quell the rioters.

The three men immediately became good friends, and returned to Zhang's house to discuss their next move. In the peach garden behind the house, they made an oath to treat each other as brothers and do everything in their power to serve the empire and its citizens.

Liu had special armoury and weapons made – two swords for himself, a crescent blade for Guan, and a steel spear for Zhang. Together they joined the provincial army.

Thanks to their courage and brilliant fighting skills, Yu Province was able to fend off the Yellow Turbans.

Although the situation in Yu Province improved for a while, the Han Empire descended further into chaos. The emperor was murdered by his servants; the young prince and the empire's political and military power fell into the hands of a warlord named Dong Zhuo. The grip of Dong's tyrannical rule was felt throughout the land.

Among those who despised Dong was Cao Cao, a distinguished army officer well known for his military genius and lack of mercy towards his enemies. He was also a brilliant leader who treated his subordinates like his family.

Cao believed he was destined for great things. Seeking a chance to seize power and fame, he joined forces with another warlord named Yuan Shao. Together they called for all the empire's governors and nobles to unite in a campaign against Dong.

One of the participants in the campaign was Sun Jian, governor of the City of Changsha in the south. Sun was an ambitious man who dreamed of being in high power. Because of this, although he was on the same side as Cao and Yuan, they deliberately withheld military support for him, and Sun was easily defeated in a battle against Dong's troops.

Meanwhile, Cao and Yuan were delighted that a new army, led by Liu, Guan and Zhang, had joined the campaign against Dong. Although the three sworn brothers were famous for their success in fighting the Yellow Turban rioters, their relatively small force was not considered a threat to Cao and Yuan.

Soon after this, Dong's troops rebelled against his tyrannical rule and murdered him. Upon hearing this news, Cao and Yuan made their move and quickly occupied Luoyang, the empire's capital. The prince, previously controlled by Dong, was now in Cao and Yuan's hands.

As part of the occupying force, Sun stationed his troops around the imperial palace in Luoyang. Knowing that Cao and Yuan loathed his company, he distanced himself by spending all his time exploring the palace and dreaming about becoming an emperor.

One moonless night, Sun noticed an eerie light glowing in a hollow behind the palace. He decided to investigate, and in the bottom of an abandoned well discovered a small, carved wooden box, which was the source of the light. He opened the box carefully, and to his amazement and joy found the imperial seal in it.

This convinced Sun that he was the rightful heir to the throne, so he decided to keep the imperial seal to himself. Cao and Yuan heard that he had found the seal and urged him to hand it over, but Sun insisted that he had never seen it.

'If I am lying,' he swore to them, 'then let me be stricken down by a thousand knives and arrows!'

Sun decided to return to Yang Province in the empire's south, his ancestral land, to establish his own kingdom there. Convinced that Sun had taken the imperial seal after all, Yuan sent his troops to capture it.

Before long, Sun was surrounded by Yuan's troops. He tried to make a dash for it, but no sooner had he made a move than he was ambushed from all sides and impaled by a thousand knives and arrows. He died instantly.

Yuan's troops searched Sun's belongings over and over for the imperial seal, but could not find it. They were forced to accept that he had not taken it. So where was the seal now?

Meanwhile, in the capital Luoyang, Cao had split up with Yuan and declared himself sole guardian of the prince. His power increased as warriors and strategists from all over the empire arrived to support him. They expected him to help the prince establish a good government and take care of the people. But Cao had something else in mind.

By this time, Liu and his two sworn brothers had retired to manage the small Pingyuan County, convinced that the empire was now in good hands. As Liu's reputation as a great leader grew, he was invited to govern the nearby Xu Province, a wealthy and strategically important area in the centre of the empire.

Never a greedy person, Liu declined the offer, but it soon became clear why Xu Province needed a strong governor. In an attempt to expand his influence yet further, Cao attacked Xu Province and started stealing crops and valuables.

Liu could not stand by and watch such aggression. He had thought that Cao was a loyal servant to the prince; now he could see that Cao was simply another warlord whose goal was to seize the empire for himself. Determined to protect the people of Xu Province from more attacks, Liu accepted their offer of governorship. Cao shifted his attention to countering his other enemies, and Xu Province was spared.

Cao now turned his attention to the capital city, Luoyang, in a bid to destroy the last of the Yellow Turban rioters. By now he was the highest-ranking military officer in the empire.

Slowly but steadily Cao placed his own people in the imperial government and banished those who refused to support him. Eventually he became so powerful that even the prince had to obey his orders. As Cao became more and more ambitious, he came to see Liu in Xu Province as a serious threat.

Always cunning and manipulative, Cao faked an order from the prince instructing Liu to conquer a rebellious warlord in a distant province. Always loyal to the empire, Liu immediately obeyed the order and left Xu Province with an army; his sworn brother Guan went with him. His other sworn brother Zhang stayed behind to look after Liu's family.

As Cao had foreseen, Xu Province was soon under attack by other warlords who were jealous of Liu's power. Although Zhang was a

brilliant warrior, he was no match for so many
invading forces. Xu Province was occupied and
Liu's family imprisoned.

Zhang managed to escape, and later
confessed to Liu and Guan what had happened.
He was so ashamed of his failure to protect Liu's
family that he tried to kill himself as punishment.

'What are you doing?' Liu scolded Zhang. 'As
my sworn brother you are as important to me
as my limbs, while my family is more like my
clothes. I can mend my clothes if they are torn,
but how can I rejoin my limbs if they are chopped
off?'

Zhang was deeply moved by Liu's kindness.
He swore that he would do all he could to rescue
Liu's family.

When Sun Jian died in Yuan Shao's ambush, the missing imperial seal was already in the hands of his eldest son Sun Ce, so it was still with the family of the man who had found it in the abandoned well.

Yuan, Cao's one-time ally, was now his bitter enemy, and needed the imperial seal more than ever to assert his power over Cao. Sun Ce wanted to return his father's body to Yang Province for a proper funeral; Yuan wanted the seal. After much negotiation, Sun Ce agreed to give Yuan the seal in exchange for safe passage for his father's remains. By possessing the imperial seal, Yuan thought he could control Sun Ce.

As soon as Sun Ce returned home to Yang Province in the empire's south, he vowed to avenge his father's violent death at the hands of Yuan's troops. His good friend Zhou Yu, a brilliant scholar and military strategist, agreed to assist him in establishing a stronghold in the south of the empire.

A smart and handsome young man in his early twenties, Zhou had studied numerous ancient teachings, and understood the importance of looking after the people. He advised Sun Ce to instruct his army not to disturb civilians. Instead of being imprisoned or killed, those conquered by Sun were given the chance either to join him or simply to retire in peace. Thus Sun's reputation as a benevolent governor grew in the south, and in time even Cao in the north began to consider him a threat.

Meanwhile, Liu had decided that the only way to stand against the warlords who wanted influence in Xu Province was to join forces with Cao. With Cao's help, he was able to drive out the warlords and free his family. This pleased Cao tremendously, for he would need all the support he could get in order to dominate the northern part of the empire and create a power base to rival Sun's stronghold in the south.

Like Sun, Cao was aware of the importance of appeasing the people, and ordered his troops not to disturb the civilian population. He took this oath very seriously. On one occasion, when his horse broke loose and dashed into a farm, damaging the crops there, he tried to kill himself as punishment, but was stopped by his strategists. Cao cut off his hair instead, this sign of repentance winning the undying respect and obedience of his troops. Gestures like this helped Cao move closer to his goal of seizing the entire empire for himself.

In the capital, Luoyang, the prince and a few of his loyal servants finally recognised Cao's ambition to steal the throne. Liu and his sworn brothers Zhang and Guan were well known for their unswerving loyalty to the empire, so the prince contacted Liu secretly to enlist his help.

Cao discovered the prince's plan, and put him under house arrest. Furious with Liu and his sworn brothers, he then launched an attack on them.

Zhang was forced to flee after his soldiers were overwhelmed, and Liu was forced to take shelter in Yuan's camp. Only Guan was left to defend Xu Province.

Desperate to keep Liu's family alive, Guan announced he would surrender to Cao on three conditions – that he would remain loyal only to the empire, that Cao would take care of Liu's family, and that he would never betray his two sworn brothers. Confident that his power and charisma were enough to win Guan over to his side and swear loyalty to him, Cao agreed.

Cao rewarded Guan with a fine set of armour. Guan put it on, but underneath it he still wore the old armour given to him by Liu. Cao also gave Guan a famous horse called Red Rabbit, a gift that delighted Guan tremendously.

'I have heard that Red Rabbit can run thousands of miles in just one day,' he said to Cao. 'It means as soon as I find out where Liu is, I can see him that very day.' Cao thus knew that Guan's allegiance to Liu could never be severed. Indeed, as soon as Guan discovered where Liu was, he left Cao's camp, taking only Liu's family and Red Rabbit, and leaving behind everything else Cao had given him.

During the escape Guan broke through five of Cao's military blockades and killed six of his

greatest warriors. Cao was very much enraged
by this, but he could not help admiring the
brilliance, determination and courage of Guan
as a great warrior.

While Guan was reunited with his two sworn brothers in the north, Sun Ce was in trouble in the south. In Yang Province, a priest who possessed powerful gifts of healing had become very popular. Sun became envious of the priest's influence; he convinced himself that the priest was practising witchcraft, and had him executed.

From that moment on, Sun Ce saw the priest's ghost following him everywhere he went.

Soon he fell gravely ill. Before he died, he named his younger brother Sun Quan as his successor. Sun Quan was just eighteen years old. He had a humble nature, and welcomed advice and criticism from those around him.

While he was a good listener, he was also determined to fulfil his father and brother's dream of establishing a strong kingdom in the south. He continued to rely on the guidance of Zhou, his brother's strategist. Taking Zhou's advice, Sun Quan decided to join forces with Cao in a military campaign against Yuan, whose troops had ambushed and murdered his father.

Cao knew that in order to dominate the northern part of the empire he had to destroy Yuan, his one-time ally. Although Cao only had an army of forty thousand men, he was confident that he could defeat Yuan's one hundred and ten thousand troops.

Cao tricked Yuan into splitting up his men, thus overwhelming many of them. His next tactic was to abandon one of his key forts and evacuate its occupants, ordering them to discard their valuables as they left. When Yuan's soldiers arrived at the fort and began gathering up the valuables, Cao's men ambushed and killed them all.

Yuan next attacked the town of Guandu, where Cao had concentrated his forces. Both sides dug trenches and tunnels to undermine each other's forces. Yuan's troops built platforms and showered Cao's men with arrows. Cao's men carried shields above their heads and retaliated with catapults, destroying Yuan's platforms. It was a battle more brutal and bloody than anyone had ever seen before.

The Battle of Guandu lasted more than nine months. Eventually one of Yuan's strategists defected to Cao's camp and informed him that Yuan had stored all of his provisions near the town of Wuchao. Cao immediately attacked Wuchao and set fire to the town, severely weakening the morale

of Yuan's army. Fearing for his life, Yuan fled and left his starving men to surrender.

In this way Cao won the Battle of Guandu, and came to dominance over the northern part of the empire. The weakened Yuan was forced to return the imperial seal to Cao, thus losing both his army and his mark of authority.

While Cao celebrated his victory in the north, Liu and his sworn brothers settled in Jing Province in the southwest of the empire. They were desperate to find a way to regain the influence they had held in Xu Province, and heard about a famous scholar named Zhuge Liang, who lived in nearby Crouching Dragon Hill. Liu decided to approach Zhuge for advice.

The first time Liu visited Crouching Dragon Hill, Zhuge was nowhere to be seen, and when Liu visited the second time Zhuge was out again. Zhang, always rather ill-tempered and reckless, volunteered to find the scholar and beat him up. 'No,' replied Liu. 'A talented scholar like Zhuge deserves proper respect.'

The third time Liu visited, Zhuge was sleeping. Liu and his sworn brothers stood waiting outside his house for many hours. Both Zhang and Guan were annoyed at what they perceived to be such rude treatment. 'Let's burn Zhuge's house down and force him out,' proposed Zhang. 'No,' said Liu. 'Where important things are to be learned, you must learn to be patient.'

At last Zhuge woke up and agreed to meet
them. As they discussed the affairs of the collapsing
empire, Zhuge advised that Liu establish a
stronghold in Jing Province in order to counter
Cao in the north and Sun Quan in the south.
Furthermore, Zhuge suggested that Liu should
befriend the native tribes in the west and southwest
of the empire while preparing for a move towards
neighbouring Yi Province's Hanzhong Region,
the heart of the empire that was both prosperous
and strategically important. Much to Liu's delight,
Zhuge agreed to be his military strategist and help
him achieve these goals.

Zhang did not think much of the plans of someone who spent as much time sleeping as Zhuge did. Soon, however, he was to witness the scholar's talents for himself.

When Cao launched another attack upon Liu in Jing Province, Zhuge asked Guan to station his men on the left-hand side of a weedy valley. Zhang's army was told to hide in the woods on the right-hand side of the valley, while Liu's men were to be at the front of the battle. 'When Cao's troops arrive,' Zhuge instructed Liu, 'you and your men should simply run away.'

'Where will you be?' Zhang challenged the scholar.

'I'll stay behind and watch,' replied Zhang, smiling.

When Cao's troops arrived, they were so eager to capture Liu that they ran towards him along the bottom of the valley. As Zhuge had instructed, Liu and his men started to run away from the attackers, whereupon Guan and Zhang led their men in an attack on Cao's forces from both sides. Liu now turned his men around to launch an attack, while Zhuge set fire to the weeds in the valley floor behind Cao, cutting off his retreat. Cao's troops were trapped, and most perished among the burning weeds.

Liu, Guan and Zhang now believed that Zhuge was indeed a brilliant military strategist. Never again would they doubt any plan he proposed.

Liu and Zhuge now travelled to Yang Province to propose an alliance with Sun Quan. Sun's strategist, the young and handsome scholar Zhou, was very wary. He had heard about Liu's reputation, and feared that Sun and his province were at great risk. He took Sun aside. 'With Zhuge's help,' he advised, 'Liu will one day become your greatest enemy. Instead of helping him, you should try to destroy him while you can.'

Zhou devised a plan to assassinate Liu, but it was interrupted by a sudden attack by Cao, who felt threatened by the proposed alliance between Liu and Sun. Zhou knew that Liu and Zhuge had travelled to Yang Province alone, without any troops or weapons, and saw a chance to humiliate them.

'I know you have no men to help counter Cao's forces,' Zhou said to Zhuge, 'but can you provide some weapons? Might you be able to supply some arrows?' He smiled to himself, knowing that Zhuge would have to admit to having nothing to offer.

'No problem,' replied Zhuge. 'I'll give you ten thousand arrows in three days' time, if you could just lend me twenty boats to carry them in.' Zhou was puzzled about where Zhuge would find so many arrows so quickly, but gave him the benefit of the doubt and lent him the boats.

Zhuge knew that Cao had stationed his

troops along the banks of the Yangtze River, so he arranged to have man-size figurines made of straw placed on the boats. He also studied the weather patterns and foresaw that on the third night it would be very foggy. At dusk on the third evening he floated the boats down the river, and shouted a warning to Cao's men. Cao thought it was an ambush, but was reluctant to send his troops out into the fog. Instead he ordered them to shower the shadowy troops on the boats with thousands of arrows. The silence from the river persuaded Cao that they had managed to dispose of every last man of Liu's army.

When the fog cleared, Zhuge beached the twenty boats on the bank of the river opposite Cao's troops. His plan had worked brilliantly, as the straw figures on the boats had collected more than ten thousand of Cao's arrows. Zhuge smiled and waved at Cao across the river. 'Thanks for your arrows!' he taunted.

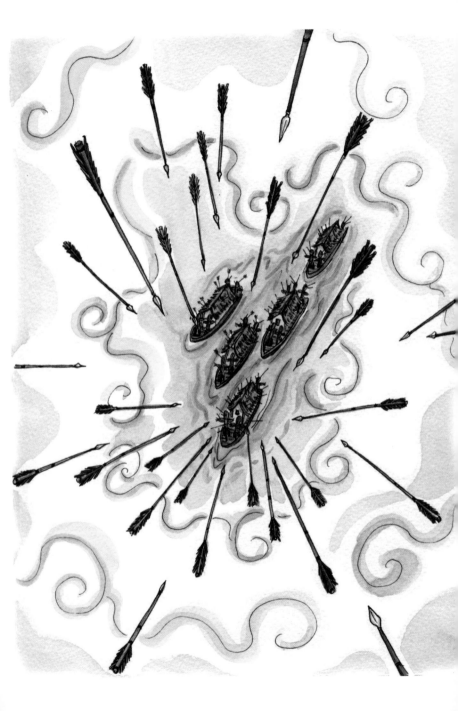

Seeing the arrows Zhuge had so easily acquired through his clever subterfuge, Zhou felt a fire of jealousy burning inside him. Across the river, Cao was grinding his teeth in anger.

Regardless of any alliance there might be between Liu and Sun, Cao determined to destroy them both and safeguard his own interests. His army was camped on the north bank of the Yangtze River opposite the Red Cliffs. He knew that in order to defeat his southern enemies, who were used to travelling by boat, he would have to fight on the river's turbulent waters.

Cao's troops came from the north of the empire, a region of hills and plains. They were ignorant of the ways of fighting on and across the wide rivers of the south. They were able to buy and steal boats to transport men and weapons, but many of them, including Cao himself, found that they suffered badly from seasickness.

Seeing his troops severely weakened by constant sickness, Cao devised a plan to stabilise the boats by securing them together with iron chains. All his vessels were shackled together, like a gigantic floating fortress. Men and horses could now walk safely over the boat fortress from end to end as if they were on dry land. Cao smiled approvingly at his own brilliance.

On the south side of the river, Zhou saw a great opportunity to attack Cao's troops with fire. However, he would be lucky if anyone could manage to set fire to even one of Cao's boats, which were all closely guarded. Even if this could be done, how could the fire be guaranteed to spread to the whole fleet? What was needed was a sure way to start the fire, and a strong easterly wind to fan the flames in the right direction, along the whole chain of boats.

Zhou hoped desperately for an easterly wind, but it did not come. As Cao's floating fortress advanced across the river, it seemed that Sun's troops were doomed. Zhou was so desperate that he fell ill.

It was Zhuge who again came to the rescue, working his magic to create a growing easterly wind. As the wind increased, he sent out a small boat with two unarmed soldiers waving a white flag to show their desire to surrender. They were allowed to moor near the floating fortress, where they quickly lit torches and threw them into one of Cao's boats. As Cao's troops rushed to douse the flames, Zhuge sent burning boats full of fatty oil and dry reeds floating down the river, which rammed into Cao's floating fortress and set it ablaze. Soon the fire, spread rapidly by the fierce wind, had consumed Cao's entire fleet. Cao only just escaped with his life.

Zhuge's triumph at the Battle of Red Cliffs made Zhou ever more bitter. He could not understand why, despite his talents and efforts, he could never outwit Zhuge. In his final battle with Cao's troops, Zhou commanded from the front line and was fatally wounded by a stray arrow. As he lay dying he still could not understand why Zhuge's powers had prevailed. 'The Heavens had already created Zhou,' he cried, 'so why was Zhuge ever born?'

Liu and Zhuge returned home to Jing Province, and asked Guan to be its governor. To avenge the death of Zhou, Sun made a treaty with Cao. He would help Cao defeat Guan and capture Jing Province, and in return would be allowed to establish the Kingdom of Wu and dominate the south.

Together Cao and Sun hatched a plan. Cao threatened to attack Jing Province, and as Guan led his army north to confront Cao's forces, Sun's men marched into Jing from the east. Cao and Sun's armies joined forces to attack Guan and his men, and Guan was captured by Sun. Sun tried to persuade Guan to switch allegiance to him, but Guan refused. He would rather die than betray his sworn brother Liu. Bravely he gave his life, and Sun's warriors bore his severed head to their master.

Sun gave Guan's head to Cao to thank him for his help. Cao was delighted, but Sun wanted Liu to blame Cao for Guan's death and the loss of Jing Province, leaving Sun free to make a pact with Liu.

Sima Yi, Cao's military strategist, saw straight through Sun's plans. Cunning and manipulative as an old fox, Sima suggested that Cao pay proper respect to Guan's remains, thus ensuring that Liu would not blame him for the loss of his sworn brother.

When he heard the news of Guan's death, Liu cried for three days until his eyes started to bleed. He vowed revenge and wanted to launch an attack on Sun, but Zhuge advised against it. 'That is exactly what Cao wants, to lure you into attacking Sun so they can both ambush you,' he cautioned.

Cao took Sima's advice and gave Guan's remains a ceremonial burial, but no sooner was Guan buried than Cao started seeing Guan's ghost every night in his dreams. Then he started seeing the ghosts of all the people he had ever killed in his pursuit of fame and power. He grew weaker and weaker, and was

forced to take to his sickbed. He knew that he did not have long to live.

The dying Cao persuaded the prince of the now defunct Han Empire to name him the ruler of Wei, an enormous region in the north with ten prosperous cities, so that his son Cao Pi would have something to inherit. Cao Pi was far from grateful, however. He was greedy for more. He knew he could not simply murder the prince and take over the empire.

Instead, he led an army to the imperial palace in Luoyang and forced the prince to renounce his throne. With a knife at his throat, the trembling prince handed over the imperial seal, returned by the defeated Yuan many years earlier.

Now the imperial seal – and all the political and military power it embodied – was in Cao Pi's hands. The Kingdom of Wei asserted its authority over the whole of the north, and the once great Han Empire was no more.

There were now two great powers in the land, Cao Pi's Kingdom of Wei in the north and Sun Quan's Kingdom of Wu in the south. Zhuge urged Liu to proclaim himself ruler of the south-western Kingdom of Shu, renaming it Shu Han and proclaiming it the one true successor to the now lost Han Empire. Zhuge also advised Liu not to take revenge on Sun.

Ever since Guan's death, his sworn brother Zhang had been weeping and drinking heavily.

The liquor could not ease his sorrow, so he lashed out at his soldiers. Their long-held respect for the great warrior slowly turned into resentment and hatred.

One day Zhang had two of his officers severely beaten because they had not polished his armour well enough. That night Zhang was drunk again, and fell asleep in his tent. The two officers sneaked in, cut off his head, and defected to Sun's camp.

Liu collapsed when he heard about the loss of Zhang. His two sworn brothers were both dead, and Liu blamed Sun for both killings. Against Zhuge's advice, Liu determined to launch an attack against the Kingdom of Wu.

Liu led his army eastward, and captured several key towns. Then he set up a chain of camps in preparation for a final attack on Sun's fortress in the town of Xiaoting.

It was summer and very hot, and the humidity from the nearby swamps and woods made the heat even more unbearable. Many of Liu's men had heatstroke. The morale in his camps fell as the soldiers suffered exhaustion and homesickness. They were further frustrated by Sun's silence; no matter how much Liu taunted Sun with curses and threats, he refused to come out of his fortress.

But finally, seeing how agitated Liu's men had become, Sun decided it was time for a counter-attack. He sent spies to encircle Liu's camps and set them on fire. The dry woods and reed beds quickly became infernos. As Liu's men rushed around trying to stop the fires, Sun's troops attacked. Nearly all of Liu's camps were destroyed as he beat a hasty retreat, protected only by a few of his most faithful officers.

Liu survived the disastrous defeat at the Battle of Xiaoting, but blamed himself for not accepting Zhuge's advice and safeguarding his men.

His shame drove him into a steep decline. Liu fell ill and died, leaving the Kingdom of Shu Han to his young son Liu Shan, under the protection of Zhuge.

When he heard of Liu's death, Cao was keen to destroy the Kingdom of Shu Han once and for all. He liaised with the native tribes who lived near Shu Han and asked them to join forces with him. Including Cao's men, there were soon five different armies on their way to invade Shu Han.

Liu Shan and his court panicked, but as usual Zhuge was quite calm. He ordered that the kingdom's borders should be strengthened with plenty of supplies, and worked with military officers at all levels to devise war plans to target each invading army. Diplomats were sent to engage the local tribes in treaties and trade. The diplomats stressed the benefits of siding with the Kingdom of Shu Han against the Kingdom of Wei.

In the end, apart from one tribe led by Meng Huo, a warrior renowned for his strength and courage, the other tribal armies agreed to retreat and switch their allegiance to the Kingdom of Shu Han. This victory of Zhuge's without bloodshed greatly upset Cao. He immediately planned an attack on the Kingdom of Wu to prevent it from helping Shu Han.

Meanwhile, Zhuge decided to teach Meng a lesson. As Meng led his tribesmen against the Kingdom of Shu Han, Zhuge defeated and captured him seven times, each time releasing him and allowing him to come back for another battle. 'Pacification of the south requires that we subdue the hearts of the local people,' Zhuge instructed his men.

By the time Meng was released the seventh time, he became a great admirer of Zhuge and

pledged alliance with the Kingdom of Shu Han.
In the years to come, Meng would remain the
most faithful ally the kingdom had ever had.

It was now that Zhuge decided to attack Cao.
The aging scholar was suffering from chronic
tuberculosis and constant stress from managing
military campaigns. He would need a few tricks
up his sleeves to confront his nemesis, Sima,
who was now Cao's most trusted strategist.

As Zhuge became increasingly ill, his troops were trapped by Sima's army near the Wuzhang Plains. Knowing that resistance would be futile, Zhuge devised a plan. He sat on the top of a nearby hill where everyone could see him, calmly playing a zither and drinking tea.

While Sima's attention was focused on Zhuge and what he was going to do next, the Shu Han troops withdrew to a safe distance. Seeing all this, Sima immediately assumed that Zhuge must have more men hiding nearby in preparation for an ambush, otherwise how could the scholar be so calm and confident when none of his troops was there to protect him? However cunning and manipulative he was, Sima could never imagine that Zhuge would confront the massed Wei forces all by himself. Believing the worst, Sima ordered a hasty retreat.

Thus the ailing Zhuge won the Battle of Wuzhang Plains without even one of his

soldiers fighting. The only casualty was the
scholar himself, whose strength and breath
finally left him.

Before Zhuge died, he ordered a wooden
statue of himself to be made. The Shu Han
troops put the statue on a cart and paraded it
before the Wei army. Seeing the statue from
a distance and mistaking it for a real person,
Sima was heard to yell in horror, 'Zhuge's still
alive! He'll get me this time!'

When his physician attended him, Sima was still trembling, his face whiter than paper. Thus it was reported that even a dead Zhuge could scare off a live Sima.

After the Battle of the Wuzhang Plains and Zhuge's death, there was virtually a stalemate between the three kingdoms – Wei in the north, Wu in the south, and Shu Han in the west. In Shu Han, Liu Shan proved to be a weak ruler without Zhuge's guidance, trusting his court to treacherous officials who had nothing better to do than fight among themselves. Eventually Shu Han was conquered by the Kingdom of Wei.

In the Kingdom of Wei, Cao died and left the throne to his son, who appointed Sima to manage the kingdom. Power went to Sima's head; he banished the Cao family's supporters, and promoted his relatives and friends to high office.

Slowly but steadily, all political and military power fell into Sima's hands. His grandson eventually forced the last Cao ruler to hand over the throne, effectively destroying the Kingdom of Wei.

In the Kingdom of Wu, Sun Quan also died, and various princes and nobles fought for the throne. Even after a new ruler was finally chosen, he turned out to be a useless tyrant. Eventually the Kingdom of Wu was conquered by Sima.

Having conquered all three kingdoms and united the land, Sima established an empire called Jin. A new dynasty thus began, and the nearly century-long legacy of the three kingdoms was no more.

TAKING THINGS FURTHER
The real read

The *Real Reads* version of *The Three Kingdoms* is a retelling in English of Luo Guanzhong's wonderful (and very long!) Chinese work. If you would like to read the full Chinese version in all its original splendour, you will need to learn the Chinese language. Otherwise you will have to rely on one of the English translations whose details you will find on page 61.

Filling in the spaces

The loss of so many of Luo Guanzhong's original words is a sad but necessary part of the shortening process. We have had to make some difficult decisions, omitting subplots and characters, some important, some less so, but all interesting. We have also, at times, taken the liberty of combining two events into one, or of giving a character words or actions that originally belong to another. The points below will fill in some of the gaps, but nothing can beat the original.

- In the original book there is much more detailed description about the Yellow Turban riots and the backgrounds of Cao Cao, Liu Bei and Sun Jian. There is also a lot more detail about Liu's gain and loss of Xu County and Sun Quan's rise to power after the deaths of his father and elder brother, as well as the Cao family being forced to renounce the throne to the Sima family, which later establishes the Jin Dynasty that unites the whole of China.

- Luo opens his book by saying (in the style typical of many Chinese sayings) 'The empire long divided must unite, long united must divide'. To support this view, he devotes many pages to describing the complex relations between Cao, Liu and Sun. Each has established alliances with the other two and later launches attacks against them, their goal being the domination of the whole of China. There is therefore no permanent friendship nor rivalry between the three leaders and their supporters. Neither is there any stereotypical hero or villain.

- There are far more battles than are described here between the troops commanded by Cao, Liu and Sun. Each appoints numerous warriors and military strategists who deploy all sorts of deceptions, frauds, trickeries and traps in their attempts to outwit each other. A wide range of weapons, machines and tactics are used, many of them invented by Zhuge Liang. While Zhuge appears to possess magical powers, other characters in the book are also depicted as being under the influences of reincarnation, karma, and supernatural forces.

- The complete book provides much more detailed description about the battles at Guandu, the Red Cliffs, Xiaoting, and Wuzhang Plains than is given here. In particular the Battle of Red Cliffs is depicted as a decisive battle at the end of the Han Dynasty, ensuring the survival of Liu and Sun and providing the foundation for the later establishment of the Kingdoms of Shu Han and Wu.

- After the Battle of Red Cliffs, Zhuge prevents Guan from pursuing the escaping Cao, concerned that Guan will spare Cao's life on account of their past friendship. Guan pledges that he is willing to face execution if he fails to kill Cao. However, Guan eventually captures and releases Cao, just as Zhuge has foreseen. When Guan returns, it is only thanks to Liu and Zhang's intervention that he is not executed. It is later revealed that Zhuge has expected Guan to spare Cao, and his intention is actually to allow Cao to escape so as to hasten the formation of the three kingdoms.

- After Liu's death, Zhuge leads five military campaigns against Cao, which are referred to as his northern expeditions. It is during the first expedition that Zhuge loses a battle in the town of Jieting and withdraws his men, then sits on top of a tower for all to see, playing a zither and drinking tea, hence scaring Sima's troops away. It is during the fifth and final expedition that Zhuge dies.

Back in time

Luo Guanzhong wrote *The Three Kingdoms* in the fourteenth century, which coincided with the defeat of the Mongols by the Chinese at the end of the Yuan Dynasty. The desire of Luo and his fellow citizens for the newly established government of the Ming Dynasty to create a civilised, strong and prosperous nation is reflected in Luo's book. It is based on events in the turbulent years near the end of the Han Dynasty and the Three Kingdoms era of China, starting in 169 CE and ending with the reunification of the nation in 280 CE.

In *The Three Kingdoms*, Luo successfully combines historical records with folk tales about the Three Kingdoms era, creating a rich tapestry of personalities. Also included in the book are materials created by previous generations of poets, writers, playwrights and composers, as well as Luo's personal interpretation of concepts such as virtue and legitimacy.

One of the things that Luo is particularly interested in is the concept of loyalty to family, friends and superiors, which is used in the book to distinguish heroes and villains. What makes characters such as Liu Bei, Guan Yu and Zhang Fei heroes is their determination and contribution to what they believe to be the right cause, rather than their actual achievements.

In *The Three Kingdoms* the Kingdom of Shu Han is depicted as the legitimate inheritor of the collapsing Han regime. This suited the political climate of Luo's times, but differs from the common view in the third century that the Kingdom of Wei was the rightful successor to the Han Empire. Despite this historical inaccuracy, the events and characters described in the book are highly convincing, as Luo's description of the characters' motives is mostly very true to those of the participants in the struggles of the period.

Throughout the centuries *The Three Kingdoms* has been so warmly embraced by Chinese readers that many fictional scenes and characters have left permanent marks in traditional Chinese culture. In particular, Guan's deeds and moral qualities have been glorified. He has long been respected as the epitome of loyalty and righteousness, and is still worshipped by Chinese people today. Some think of him as the God of War, while others build shrine in their homes, shops and restaurants and honour him as a guardian.

Finding out more

We recommend the following English books and websites to gain a greater understanding of Luo Guanzhong and his writing:

Books

- Moss Roberts (trans.), *Three Kingdoms*, Beijing: Foreign Language Press, 2006. This is a complete translation of the Chinese novel in three volumes.

- Moss Roberts (trans.), *Three Kingdoms: A Historical Novel*, University of California Press, 1999. This is an abridged translation of the Chinese novel.

- Kimberly Ann Besio and Constantine Tung (eds.), *Three Kingdoms and Chinese Culture*, State University of New York Press, 2008.

Websites

- http://kongming.net/novel/intro/
A useful article by Jonathan Wu titled 'Romance of the Three Kingdoms'.

- http://kongming.net/novel/
A storehouse of *Three Kingdoms* related material.

- http://en.wikipedia.org/wiki/Romance_of_the_three_kingdoms
The Wikipedia page about *The Three Kingdoms*, with links to other pages about the novel's author and main characters.

- www.youtube.com/watch?v=PentanEzDcY
Part one, episode one, of *Yokoyama Mitsuteru Sangokushi*, a Japanese anime series based on the Chinese novel.

Food for thought

Here are some things to think about if you are reading *The Three Kingdoms* alone, or ideas for discussion if you are reading it with friends.

In retelling *The Three Kingdoms* we have tried to recreate, as accurately as possible, Luo Guanzhong's original plot and characters. We have also tried to imitate aspects of his style. Remember, however, that this is not the original work; thinking about the points below, therefore, can help you begin to understand Luo Guanzhong's craft. To move forward from here, turn to the abridged or full-length English translations of *The Three Kingdoms* and lose yourself in his wonderful storytelling.

Starting points

- Which character interests you the most? Why?

- What do you think of the three major forces that later become the Kingdoms of Wei, Shu Han and Wu? Do your feelings towards them change as you read on? How?

- Cao Cao, Liu Bei and Sun Quan are all brilliant leaders. Which one is your favourite? Why?

- If Luo Guanzhong was writing today, what technologies might he include to help the three kingdoms defeat each other in the battles mentioned in the book?

Themes

What do you think Luo Guanzhong is saying about the following themes in *The Three Kingdoms*?

- loyalty
- determination
- courage
- teamwork
- self-confidence

Style

Can you find paragraphs containing examples of the following?

- a character exposing his true character through something he says or the way he behaves
- descriptions of setting and atmosphere
- the use of a simple sentence to achieve a particular effect

Look closely at how these paragraphs are written. What do you notice? Can you write a paragraph in the same style?